EFFIE'S IMAGE

BY
N.L. Sharp

ILLUSTRATED BY
Dorothia Rohner

The author would like to thank the many writers who lent an eye and an ear to this
story on its way to final draft, including Karla Wendelin, Jean Patrick, Pat Gedbaw
and her fifth grade students, Nona Morrison, Kathy Crable, my Fremont writers' group,
and my colleagues in the Nebraska Chapter of the Society of Children's Book Writers
and Illustrators. Your help was invaluable!

The illustrator would like to thank Helenmarie, Catie, and the students and staff at
St. Paul's Lutheran Church and School in Arlington for posing as models for the
illustrations in the book. Your patience was greatly appreciated!

Published by Prairieland Press
PO Box 2404
Fremont, NE 68026-2404
Printed in U.S.A.

Book design by Lynn Gibney
The text of this book is set in 15-point Goudy Old Style.
Illustrations created in watercolor and colored pencil.

Hardcover 10 9 8 7 6 5 4 3 2 1
Softcover 10 9 8 7 6 5 4 3 2 1
First Edition

Library of Congress Cataloging-in-Publication Data
Sharp, N. L.
Effie's Image / by N.L. Sharp ; illustrated by Dorothia Rohner. --1st ed.
p. cm.
SUMMARY: An elderly woman finds new meaning for her
life when she volunteers at an elementary school.
Audience: Ages 4-8.   LCCN 2004097145
Hardcover ISBN-10: 0-9759829-5-8, Hardcover ISBN-13: 978-0-9759829-5-2
Softcover ISBN: 978-0-9759829-2-1

1. Older women--Juvenile fiction. 2. Older volunteers--Juvenile fiction.
3. Meaning (Psychology)--Juvenile fiction.
[1. Older women--Fiction. 2. Older volunteers--Fiction.
3. Meaning (Psychology)--Fiction.]
I. Rohner, Dorothia. II. Title.
PZ7.S5316Eff 2005   [E]   QBI04-800107

For every person who volunteers his or her time and
talents to help others, and most especially for Hazel.
—N. L. S.

For Mom, who taught me to quietly persevere,
Dad, who taught me to value beauty and art,
Caleb and Winston for making me laugh, and
Homer for your continuing love and support.
—D. R.

The morning Effie Armstrong turned eighty-two years old, she pushed herself out of bed.

She picked up a framed photograph and traced the image with her finger. "Effie," she said, "you're as lovely as ever."

But when she stared at herself in the
mirror, she knew it wasn't true. Her hair was
no longer black and curly. Her skin was no
longer silky and smooth. And her stooped back could not hold her body straight.

"Those days are gone," she said.
And Effie took herself back to bed.

Effie moped around her house for so long
that friends and neighbors began to worry.
Then one day, there was a knock at the door.

"Amanda Jaymes! What brings
you here so early in the morning?"
Effie asked.

"I brought Boots over to keep you
company while I'm at school."

Before Effie could say a word, the kitten jumped out of Amanda's arms. He disappeared under the sofa, and Amanda disappeared out the door.

At three o'clock, Amanda was back. "Did you and Boots have a good time?" she asked.

"No, we did not," Effie said. "He has scratched my piano. He has tangled my tatting. He has even helped himself to my bowl of ice cream."

"That cat is nothing but a nuisance. Please, take him home NOW!"

"My dad needs some help down at the church," Amanda said, the next time she came to visit. "I told him you would be perfect."

So Effie put on her walking shoes and headed for the church. She scooted around in the soft blue rolling chair. She swapped recipes with the janitor. She watered the plants and shared secrets with the mailman.

But then things started to go wrong. The copy machine
jammed. The computer would not turn on. And the telephone
with ten buttons rang and rang.

"This job is not for me,"
said Effie. "I'm going home."

"Maybe you should go to school," said Amanda.

"School!" said Effie. "Now why would I want to go to school?"

"Because it's fun. You get to read and write and draw pictures. You can even eat there."

"Imagine that," Effie muttered. "An old lady like me at school. Whoever heard of such a crazy idea."

But the more she thought about it, the more she liked it. So the next morning, dressed in her best sweater and her fanciest tatted necklace, Effie met Amanda at the corner and walked with her to school.

After stopping in the office to say good morning, they headed for Amanda's classroom.

"Welcome, Effie!" said Miss Carter. "I hope you don't mind if I put you to work."

"Of course not," said Effie. "That's why I'm here."

Effie went to work immediately. She listened to stories. She played math games.
She admired wiggly teeth and tied shoelaces. Before she knew it, it was time for lunch.

"What's that I smell?" Effie asked.

"Chicken soup and cinnamon rolls," Amanda said.

"Good," said Effie. "I'm starved." Effie was on her second cinnamon roll when the third grade teacher saw her. She asked Effie to stay and listen to the stories her students had written.

And just as Effie and Amanda were leaving, the fifth grade teacher caught her. He invited Effie back the next day to watch a video his students had made.

"Imagine that," Effie said. "Fifth graders making movies. I'll definitely be here for that." And she was. In fact, Effie walked to school with Amanda every day that week.

Soon one week became two weeks and two weeks became a month. Some days she went home at noon, and some days she stayed the whole day. She played the piano, taught the teachers how to tat, and showed the students how to make homemade ice cream.

They taught her how to run a copy machine, turn on a computer, and answer a telephone with ten buttons. Before long, no one could remember a time when Effie wasn't a regular part of every school day.

One day in May, the principal called everyone to the gym. "What's going on?" Effie asked the cooks as she passed them in the hall. "This sounds important."

"It is. You don't want to miss this."

When all the students were seated on the floor, the principal began to speak. "This year, a new friend joined our school community. She's not a student or a teacher, but every day she's here, helping in every way she can. Effie Armstrong, would you please come forward?"

Effie looked around. Everyone was smiling. Amanda grabbed her hand. "Come on," she whispered. "They're waiting for you."

Together they walked to the front of the room. The principal handed a wrapped package to Amanda. Amanda, in turn, handed it to Effie. "This is for you," she said. "Because you make every day a great day at school."

Effie opened the present and took out a framed photograph. In the picture, she was reading a book to the students in Miss Carter's classroom. Her back was softly bowed. Her cheeks were wrinkled, and her gray hair was falling out of its bun.

Effie traced the image with her finger. Effie, she thought, you're as lovely as ever. And when she stared at the sea of faces smiling back at her, she knew that it was true.